# Olly & Lilly

## Huge thanks to:

Firstly, I'd like to thank my wonderful sons, to whom I dedicate this book and who inspired me to write it. Your love, resilience, fun and determination shines through and you bring so much joy to our lives.

To my amazing husband, sharing so many special years together, my soulmate and my pillar - without you I would be incomplete.

To my family and friends. To name but a few, my Dad and late Mum, Julie W, Jackie, Dave, Alison, Sarah H, Craig, Sarah L, Bernice, Nirmala, Amanda, Julie M, Alison F, Gabs, Margaret, Ron, Clare, Fran and Lucy. To the various professionals involved in our adoption process. Amy, Alison, Estelle, Heidi, and the wonderful foster carers Jill and Keith. The work you all do humbles me.

To Lucie for helping to make my vision come to life and Fi and Books for choosing my story and for their amazing help throughout.

First published in UK in 2020 by Fiona Woodhead from FiandBooks.com
67 The Hollins, Triangle, Halifax, West Yorkshire. HX6 3LU.
www.fiandbooks.com

ww.fiandbooks.com

MAD MARCH BOOK SUBMISSION WINNER

Olly and Lilly were two young bikes. They were not just ordinary bikes, they were special off-road bikes who had a dream of becoming the fastest racing champions in the world!

They had the best wheels, the shiniest chains, the comfiest seats and the biggest smiles.

Olly and Lilly loved whooshing through muddy puddles, scrambling down rocky tracks and whizzing through leafy green forests.

Their super-speedy races always made them laugh and grin from handlebar to handlebar.

Olly and Lilly lived with Mummy Bike in their cosy home garage. Mummy looked after them with lots of love and giggles.

She did a wonderful job of keeping them safe, warm and clean even though they loved being splattered with mud and getting leaves all over their seats.

One day Olly and Lilly noticed that Mummy Bike had started to look tired and a little bit sad.

As the weeks went by, Mummy Bike stopped working properly. Her wheels couldn't spin, her brakes didn't work and her chain became very rusty.

Olly and Lilly tried to make Mummy feel better, but she found it hard to look after them. They couldn't go outside or race through the forest which made them feel very sad. Sometimes they felt cold, hungry and lonely.

4

Olly and Lilly enjoyed going to bike school where they had lots of friends and lovely teachers. Their favourite lessons were speed maths, wheel science and tyre literacy.

Normally Mummy Bike zoomed them to school and whooshed them home again, but when she was broken, she didn't want to leave their home garage. Olly and Lilly couldn't go to bike school anymore.

They missed their teachers and felt very sad that they couldn't race in the playground or do wheelies with their friends. The young bikes were confused. They didn't understand why they had to stay in their home garage all day.

Olly asked Lilly "Have we done something wrong?" but Lilly just shrugged sadly because she didn't know the answer.

6

One day a kind Yellow Helper Bike noticed that Olly and Lilly were not being looked after properly. She saw that their frames were very dirty, their tyres need pumping up and their chains were rusty. She also noticed that their smiles had disappeared.

When she visited their home garage, she found that Mummy Bike wasn't working properly and the two young bikes didn't feel like racing. She was very sad to find out that they were often left alone and hungry.

The Yellow Helper Bike wanted to help Olly, Lilly and Mummy Bike. She could see that Mummy was trying very hard and loved her young bikes very much, but Mummy couldn't give Olly and Lilly all the care they needed to be strong and happy.

The Yellow Helper Bike thought that Olly and Lilly should move to a special helper garage where they would be looked after, so she spoke to a wise Judge Bike and he agreed.

Olly and Lilly moved into the special helper garage which was clean, warm and very friendly. The helper bikes were very kind, but Olly and Lilly felt worried about leaving their home and missing Mummy Bike.

At night they whispered to each other about their dream of becoming a world-class-racing-team. They felt very helpless but they were also glad that they had each other.

In the helper garage Olly and Lilly had wonderful racing areas and endless tools but they didn't feel happy. The friendly helper bikes didn't know how to look after off-road bikes and their new parts didn't fit properly. Lilly hugged Olly and cried "Why doesn't anyone know how to look after us? It's so unfair!"

After a few days the Yellow Helper Bike came to visit Olly and Lilly. She noticed that their bike parts were all wrong and they looked unhappy. She gave them a kind smile and decided to move the young bikes to a new helper garage.

Olly and Lilly felt at home straight away in the second helper garage. The kind helper bikes knew how to look after off-road bikes, and they had all the right parts to get Olly and Lilly working again.

Their chains were oiled, their tyres were filled with air and their frames were polished until they shone.

The young bikes were warm and happy. They were shown how to clean their muddy saddles and look after their own wheels. The helper bikes taught them how to race, how to zoom off-road safely and how to stay upright on tricky bike tracks. They helped them to ride so well that they no longer needed their stabilisers.

Olly and Lilly knew that this helper garage was only a pit-stop before they found a new forever-race-team, but their smiles returned and they started to love racing again!

Meanwhile, in a nearby town, there were two grown-up bikes who dreamt of creating their own race-team-family. The two bikes were strong, fun and super-fast at off-road racing.

They both wished that they could find two speedy, nimble young bikes to join them for racing adventures. Their dream was to create a happy bike family and become the fastest race-team in the world.

The Yellow Helper Bike met with the two grown-up bikes to see where they lived and find out what sort of bikes they were. She quickly realised that they were perfect for Olly and Lilly!

A few days later she visited the young bikes to tell them all about their possible new forever-race-team. Olly and Lilly grinned. They couldn't wait to meet them. Thanks to the help and kindness from the helper garage, Olly and Lilly felt ready to move to a new home garage.

They both still really missed Mummy Bike and wished that they could see her, but they felt an excited-nervous feeling about meeting the two grown-up bikes.

Everybody was very excited when the grown-up bikes came to visit Olly and Lilly. It made them all grin from handlebar to handlebar.

They took the young bikes out for wonderful day trips where they went racing, riding, laughing and having lots of fun together. They splashed through puddles, whizzed down muddy paths and zoomed through forests feeling full of happiness.

They all liked each other very much. The grown-up bikes thought Olly and Lilly were excellent racers! Olly and Lilly moved out of the helper garage to live with the grown-up bikes and became part of their new forever-race-team.

It felt a bit strange at first, but soon the young bikes felt very happy, safe and settled in their new home garage. Everyone felt certain that this winning race-team would be together forever!

Over the coming months the family got to know each other even better. Olly and Lilly started at a fantastic new bike school and they all enjoyed learning how to race faster together. The four happy bikes went out every weekend to race speedily through fields and forests over tracks and pathways.

Olly loved to shout "wheeeeeeeeeeee!" as he zoomed along, and Lilly would answer with a loud "yippppeeeeeeee!" while the two grown-up bikes grinned - they all loved racing together. When Olly or Lilly fell over, the grown-up bikes picked them up. If the young bikes felt sad, the grown-ups comforted them. When they were tired from a day of racing the grown-up bikes carried them home.

One day the grown-up bikes spotted a poster saying that the annual Champions of the World Race was coming to town. They decided to enter as a family so that their speedy forever-race-team could race against the best bikes in the world!

As race day approached their wheels were pumped with air, chains were freshly oiled and new comfy seats were fitted. Olly and Lilly were doing wheelies with excitement. They would go to bed whispering "do you really think we can win?" and doing imaginary wheel-spins in their sleep.

Finally, the big moment came, it was race day! The four bikes were so excited that they woke up with a funny tickling feeling deep inside their bellies. They had been working so hard, they all believed that they could win the Champions of the World Race!

As they lined up to start the race, the competitors all smiled and wished each other luck. The grown-up bikes whispered to Olly and Lilly "Let's make sure we have the best fun ever. Even if we don't win... we've done this together as a family-race-team!" All the bikes were ready and giddy with excitement... then bang! The starting gun fired, and everyone raced off!

The race was tricky. It had steep turns, muddy paths and some massive jumps. At one point the family-race-team thought they were going to lose, but with some extra pedal power, a boost of energy and some encouraging shouts of "yippeeeee!" the four bikes pushed into first place just before the finish line.

Olly and Lilly felt pure happiness and excitement burst from their handlebars. They had won! Their new family-race-team could take on the world and win every race. The World Championship Gold Cup was theirs!

Olly and Lilly felt like their dream had come true. They were part of a world winning forever-race-team and they had all the care, love and parts they needed to grow up strong and happy.

The two young bikes sometimes really missed Mummy Bike, but they knew that the grown-up bikes would always be there to help them.

Olly and Lilly proudly grinned at the grown-up bikes as they conquered the steepest tracks, splashed through the deepest puddles and scrambled skilfully down the rockiest paths.

**Off-road racing as a family was their favourite thing and nothing made them happier.**

# About the author

Matt is a father of two adopted sons.

He writes about adoption on his blog **fromsoftwaretosoftplay.com** and came up with the idea of Olly and Lilly when he realised that many other books about adoption were aimed at a younger age group which didn't suit his own family.

Matt's Olly and Lilly book series encourages children of all ages and situations to talk about their feelings and face things they may feel worried about. Through his storytelling Matt hopes to help children explore and understand the fears and emotions that can arise with key life events.

Matt attends primary schools with his book series to bring his stories to life and work alongside teachers, parents and pupils to explore emotions and recognise the importance of understanding our own feelings.

Matt was diagnosed with Multiple Myeloma in 2017 and encourages everyone to register as a stem cell donor. To find out more visit **www.myeloma.org.uk**